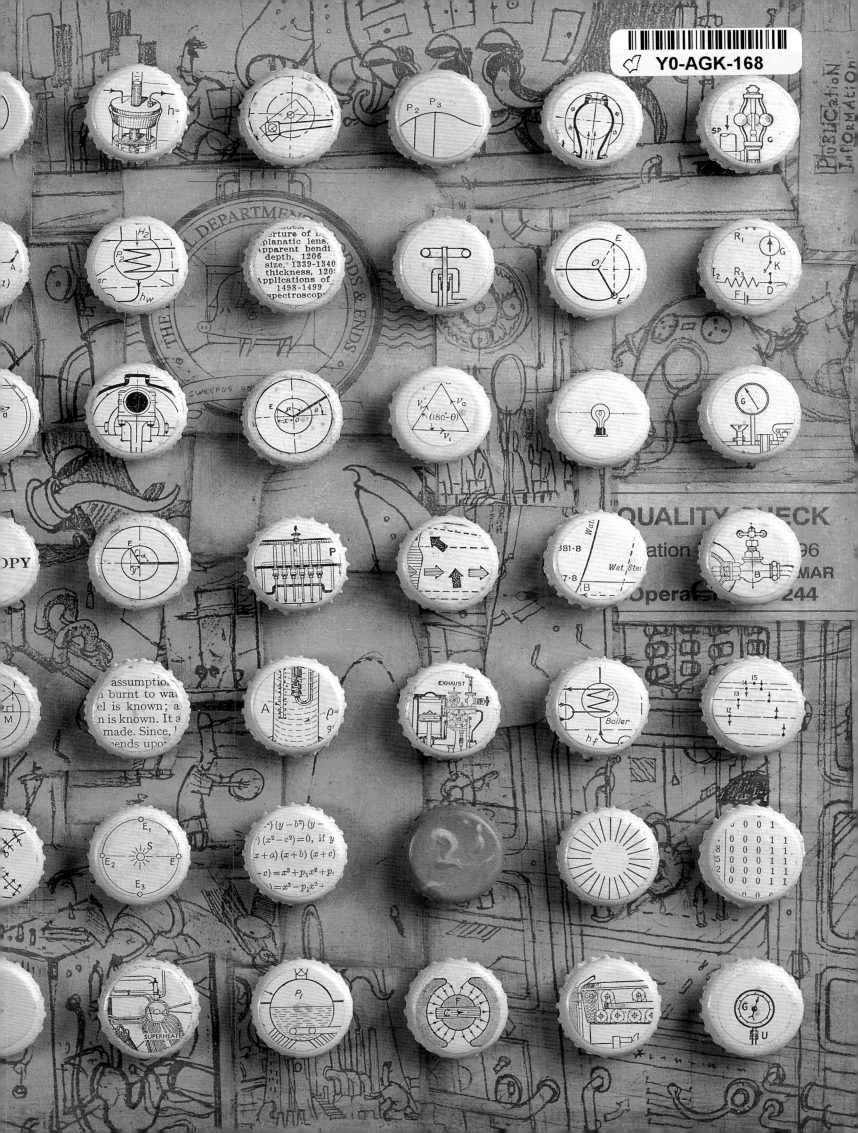

PREFACE

THIS book is intended to serve as an introductory text-book for students preparing for first examinations in the subject of heat engines and applied thermodynamics.

BUY SENSIBLE SHOES

COMFORTABLE AND RELAXED

OFFICE USE ONLY

1   Title

THE LOST Thing

FOUND BY

SHAUN TAN

INSPECTED BY
Helen #264
EDITORIAL TECHNICIAN

Lothian BOOKS

PUBLICATION INFORMATION

A Lothian Children's Book

Published in Australia and New Zealand
by Hachette Livre Australia Pty Limited
Level 17, 207 Kent Street
Sydney NSW 2000
Website: www.hachettechildrens.com.au

copyright © Shaun Tan 2000

first published 2000
reprinted 2001 (twice), 2007
paperback edition first published 2001
reprinted 2002, 2004, 2005, 2006 (twice), 2007, 2008
this paperback edition first published 2008

This book is copyright. Apart from any fair dealing
for the purposes of private study, research, criticism
or review permitted under the Copyright Act 1968, no
part may be stored or reproduced by any process
without prior written permission. Enquiries should
be made to the publisher.

NATIONAL LIBrARY OF AUSTRALIA
CatalOguing-in-Publication data:

Tan, Shaun
   The lost thing.

   ISBN 978 0 7344 0074 1.
   ISBN 978 0 7344 1088 7. (paperback)

   1.Title

   A823.3

Design by Shaun Tan
colour reproduction by Scott Digital, Port Melbourne
Printed in China by Everbest Printing Co Ltd

illustration media: acrylic, oils; Dad's Old physics+engineering text-books, some bottle-tops & glue

AUTHORISATION

THE FEDERAL DEPARMENT OF INFORMATION
?
ignorare regulatum

This book is the legal property of:

Bhut Jolokia

PLEASE PRINT CLEARLY

FINGERPRINT ID

REALITY 47

LOST

OSCILLATING MAGNET

Coefficient of Correlation . 31.27.
The Standard Deviation

FUNCTIONS

HIGHER ALGEBRA.

AND SIMPLE APPLICATIONS

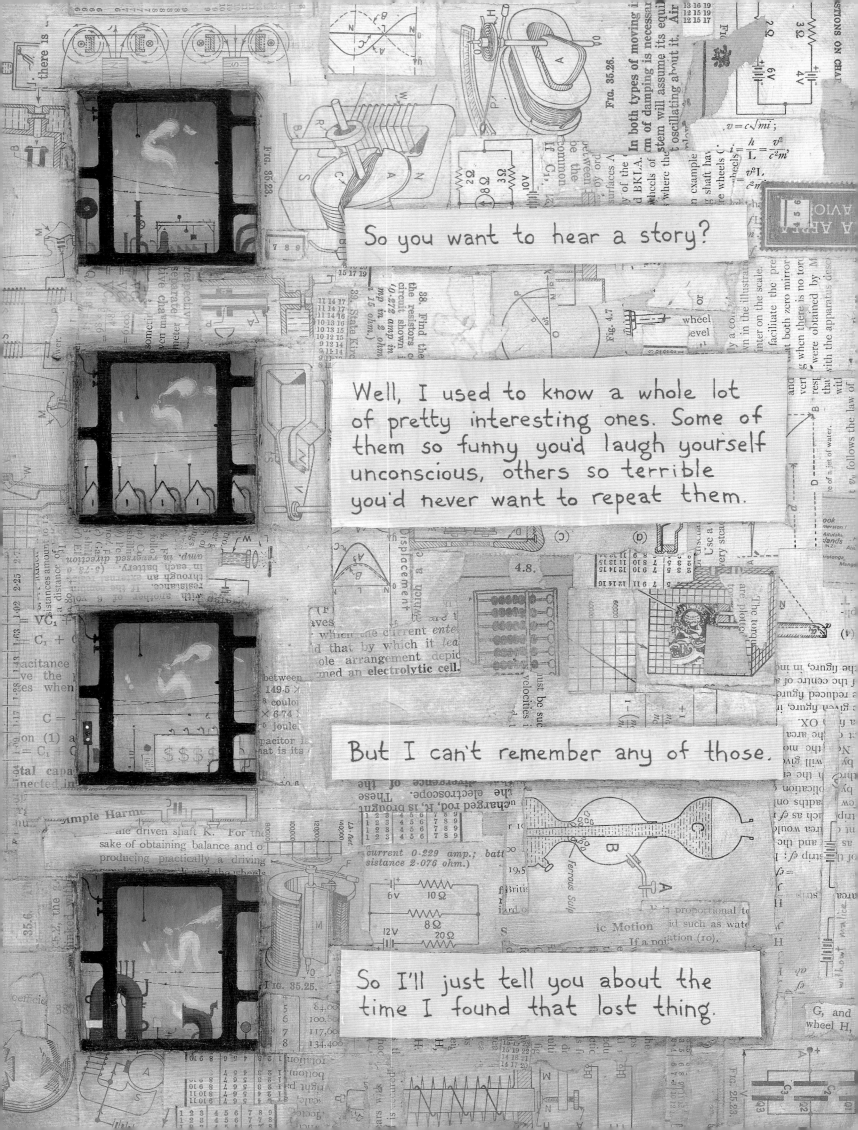

So you want to hear a story?

Well, I used to know a whole lot of pretty interesting ones. Some of them so funny you'd laugh yourself unconscious, others so terrible you'd never want to repeat them.

But I can't remember any of those.

So I'll just tell you about the time I found that lost thing.

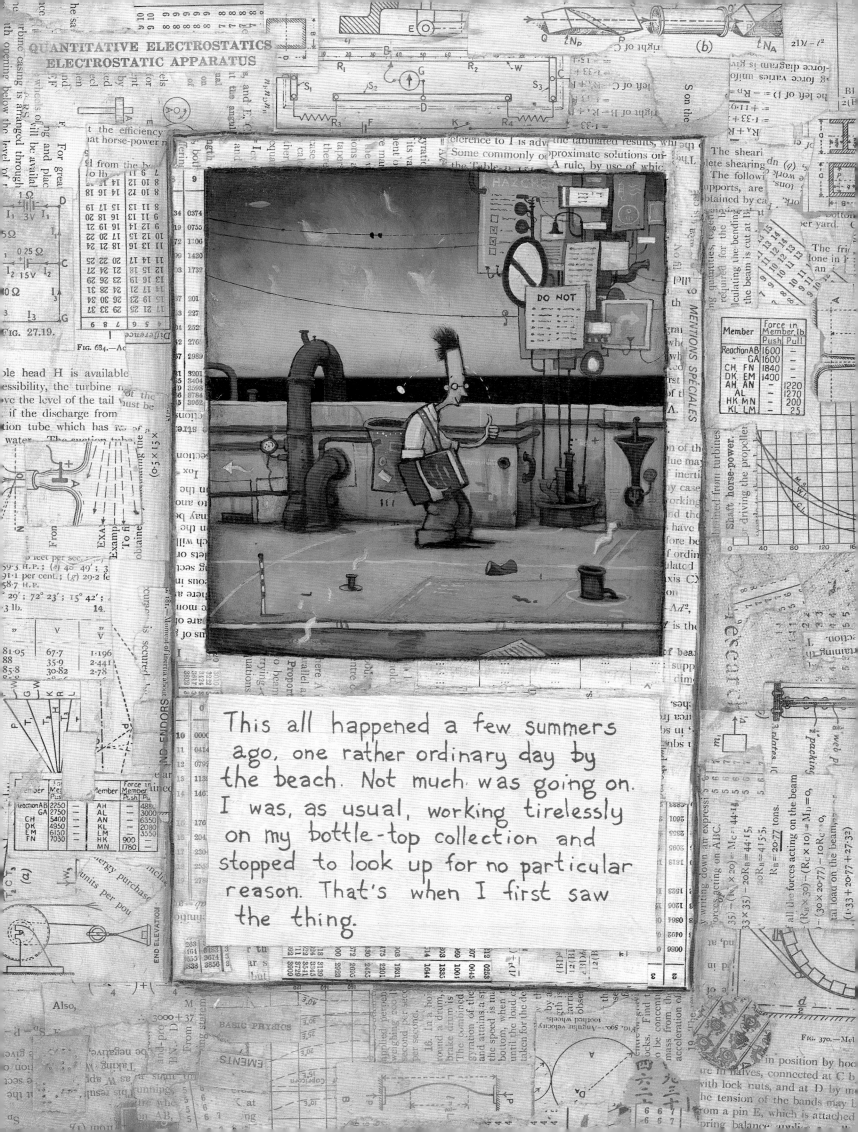

This all happened a few summers ago, one rather ordinary day by the beach. Not much was going on. I was, as usual, working tirelessly on my bottle-top collection and stopped to look up for no particular reason. That's when I first saw the thing.

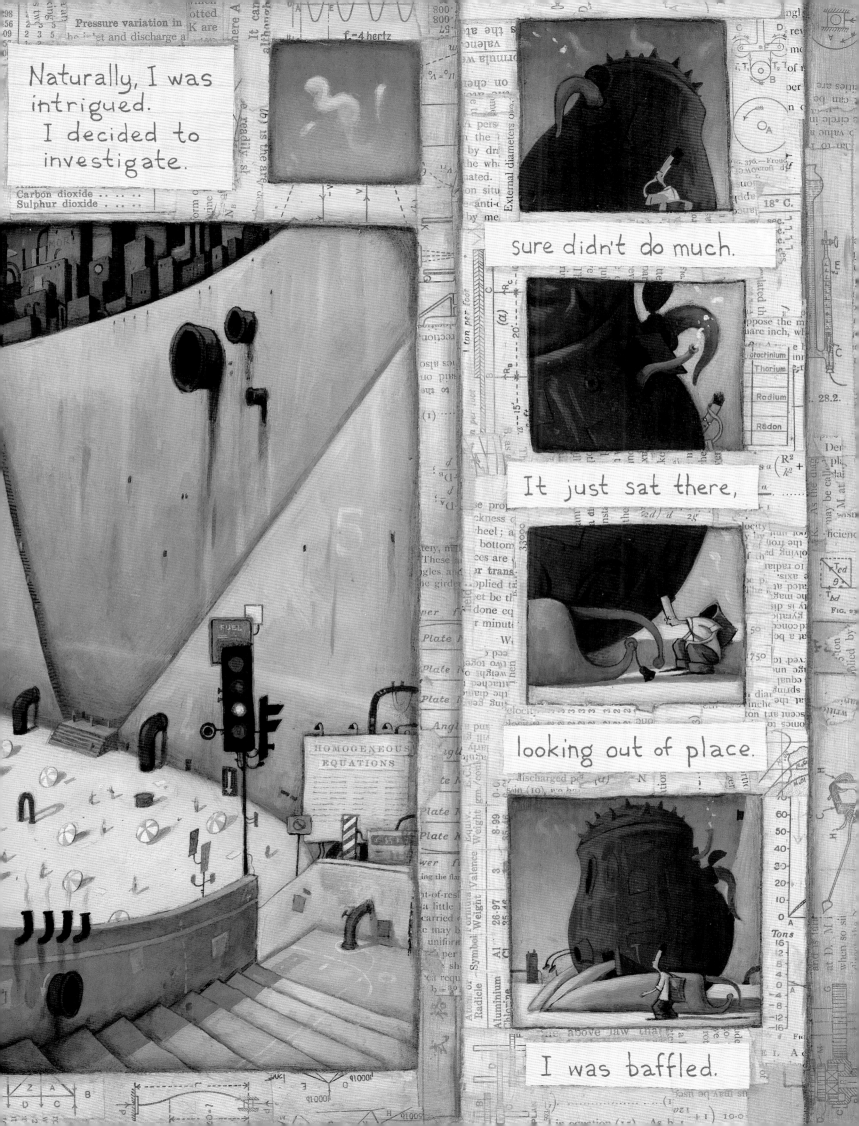

It was quite friendly though, once I started talking to it.

ANTI-LOGARITHMS

I played with the thing for most of the afternoon. It was great fun, yet I couldn't help feeling that something wasn't quite right.

Exercise 7b*

MAGNETISM

As the hours slouched by, it seemed less and less likely that anybody was coming to take the thing home. There was no denying the unhappy truth of the situation. It was <u>lost</u>.

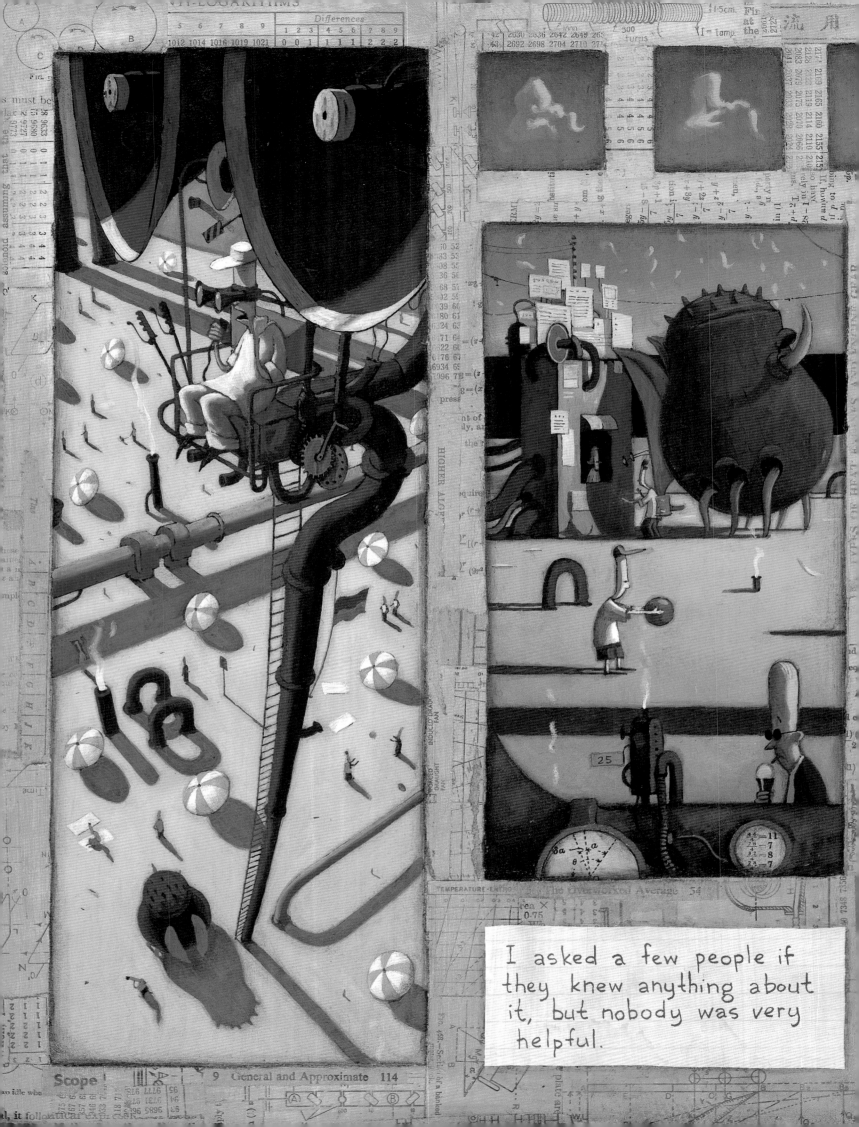

I asked a few people if they knew anything about it, but nobody was very helpful.

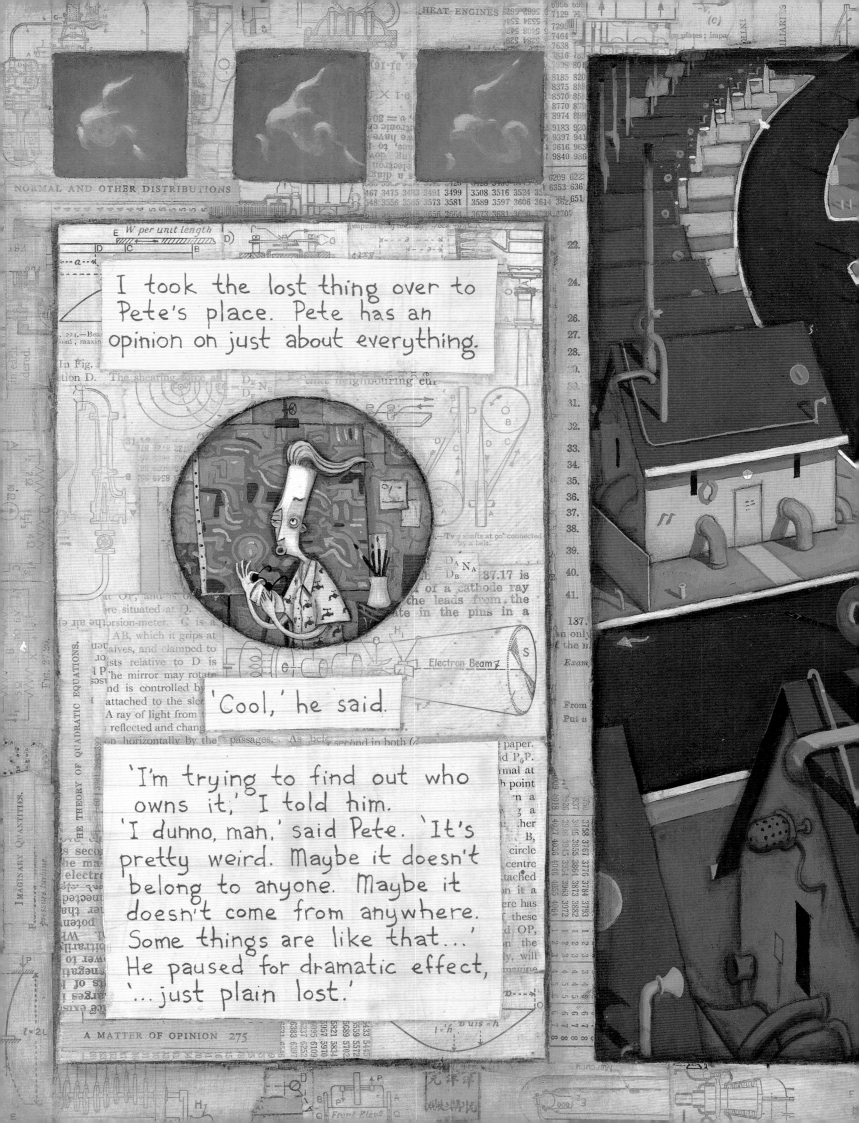

I took the lost thing over to Pete's place. Pete has an opinion on just about everything.

'Cool,' he said.

'I'm trying to find out who owns it,' I told him.
'I dunno, man,' said Pete. 'It's pretty weird. Maybe it doesn't belong to anyone. Maybe it doesn't come from anywhere. Some things are like that...'
He paused for dramatic effect,
'...just plain lost.'

underside of the piston
as, in this position, a through
assage to exhaust which may
d into the atmosphere if the

INDETERMINATE EQUATIONS OF THE FIRST DEGREE.

My parents didn't really notice it at first.
Too busy discussing current events, I guess.

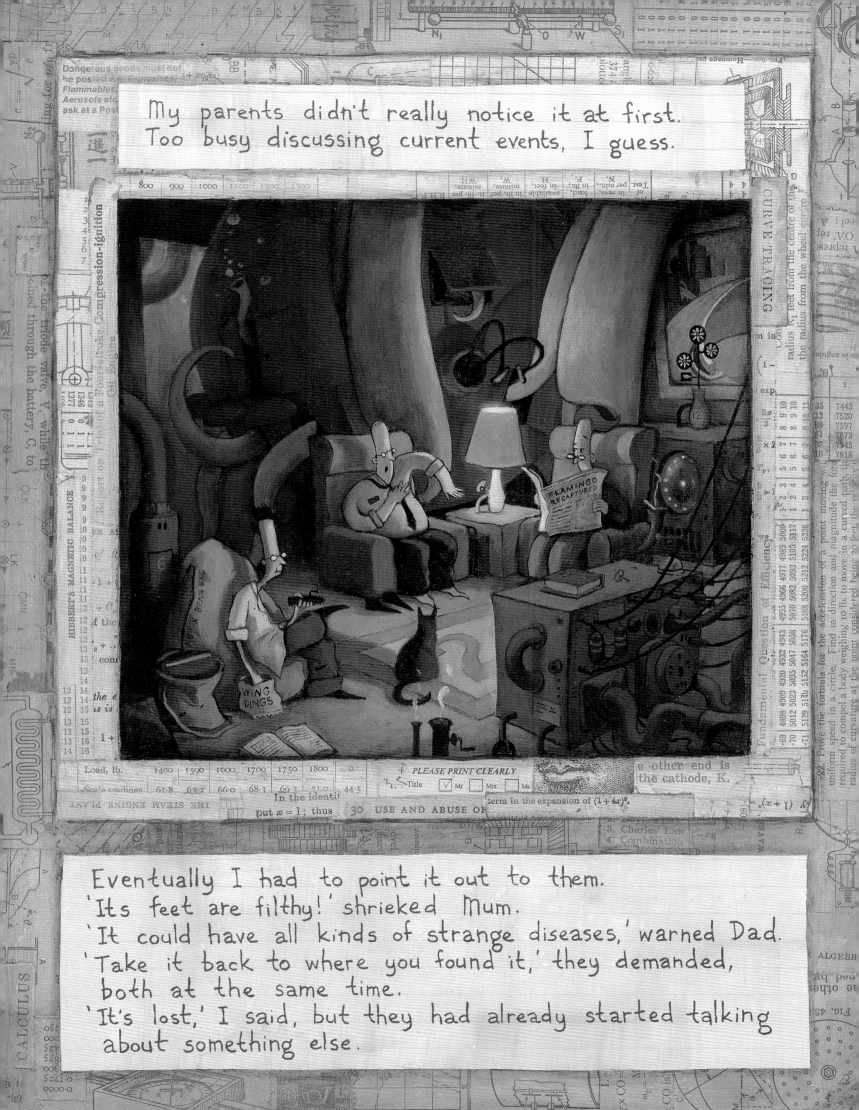

Eventually I had to point it out to them.
'Its feet are filthy!' shrieked Mum.
'It could have all kinds of strange diseases,' warned Dad.
'Take it back to where you found it,' they demanded,
both at the same time.
'It's lost,' I said, but they had already started talking
about something else.

I hid the thing in our back shed and gave it something to eat, once I found out what it liked. It seemed a bit happier then, even though it was still lost.

I checked the local paper for any lost pet notices, but only found a lot of good deals on refrigerator repairs. I remember thinking then that Pete was probably right, that some things were just plain lost. In any case, I sure couldn't keep the thing in the shed forever. Mum or Dad would eventually notice it when they came out looking for a hammer or something.

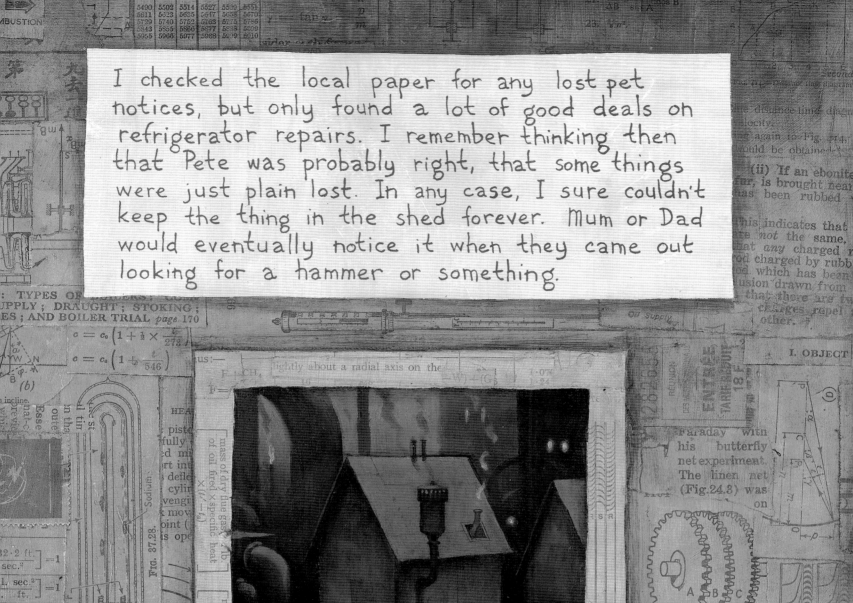

It was a real dilemma.

I was wondering what to do when a small advertisement on the last page of the paper happened to catch my eye.

bureaucritae opacus.

...GEMENT

5433 5443 54..
5559 5572 5585 559.
5689 5702 5715 57..
5821 5834 5848 5..
5957 5970 5984
6095 6109 6124.
6237 6252 6266.

0.2676	1.7968
0.2762	1.7884
0.2836	1.7884
0.2906	1.7807

Double sided for extra adhesion and durable enough to withstand the toughest bureaucratic exercises. No office desk is complete without a good spool of 20mm industrial-strength Red Tape. ORDER NOW!!!

THE FEDERAL DEPARTMENT OF ECONOMICS

consumere ergo sum.

We understand that at the end of the [day]
all that matters is the balance sheet.

...ODUCT RECALL

...potentially lethal
[fa]ult has been identi-
[f]ied in all model 350A
[D]eluxe "Suck & Slice"
[a]utomated beet-cutters
[p]urchased before June
[1]5, around 2:23pm.
Return for replacement
at your local Product
Recall Depot, with ap-
propriate appliance
receipt & registration
forms. The Federal De-
partment of Automated
Appliances apologises
for any inconvenience.

622/8

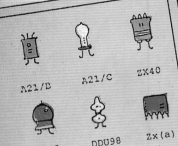

A21/B	A21/C	ZX40
UXB42	DDU98	Zx(a)
RF5(a)	TYX23	HU84-C	GL56

[Co]mmunity Service Announcement

...NOW YOUR DIODES

ARE **YOU** FINDING THAT THE ORDER OF DAY-TO-DAY LIFE IS UNEXPECTEDLY DISRUPTED BY

OBJECTS
WITHOUT
NAMES?

UNCLAIMED
PROPERTY?

TROUBLESOME
ARTIFACTS OF
UNKNOWN
ORIGIN?

FILING
CABINET
LEFTOVERS?

THINGS THAT
JUST DON'T
BELONG?

DON'T PANIC!

We've got a pigeon hole to stick it in.

DAY OR NIGHT CALL OUT MOBILE VISUAL TECHNICIANS

Instant, on-the-spot compositional solutio[ns]

* No location too obscure!

* No client too irritating!

* No plumbing too hard to draw!

Can't seem to find a
C56/b transistorised
regulator with match-
ing field coil rotor
when you need one?

YOU'RE IN LUCK

Quality Sprockets

SMITH & SMITH

Sprocketing Parts

Flywheels, gears, sprocke[ts]
wind-up things, fan belt[s]
hard-to-find alternato[rs]

Look for the Giant Gyro
southbound expressway 54...

THE FEDERAL DEPARTMENT OF ODDS & ENDS

sweepus underum carpetae.

Downtown,
6328th Street
Tall Grey Building #357b

...DEPARTMENT OF TUBES & PIPES

plumbiferus ductus.

Latest Twin
Piston Exhaust
Valves now
available!

HAVE you any perpetual-motion
ideas? If so, send them in
with a short explanation of how
they are supposed to operate.
For each one accepted and published, $5.00 will be paid. Selec-
tions will also be made from mate-
rial which has been entered in
this contest. A new Perpetual-
[Pr]oblem Contest will be...

REMEMBER:

DON'T SIGN ANY AUTOMATED APPLIANCE
CLEARANCE PERMIT UNTIL YOU'VE RE-
GISTERED AN APPLICATION FOR
HYDRAULIC TUBE FITTING IN ACCORD-
ANCE WITH BYLAW 32b OF THE OFFICE
OF MOTOR CALIBRATION'S SERVICE CODE.
And don't forget to fasten your wingnuts.

The next morning we caught a tram into the city.

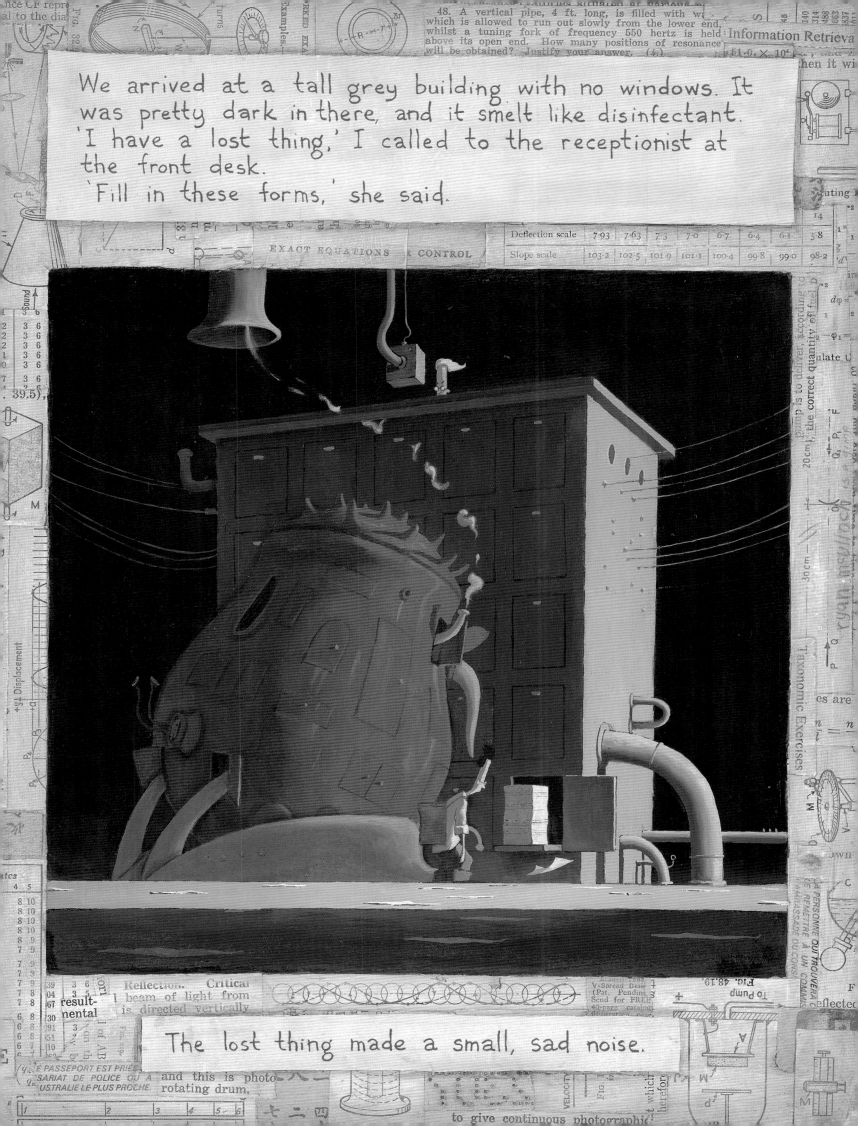

The lost thing made a small, sad noise.

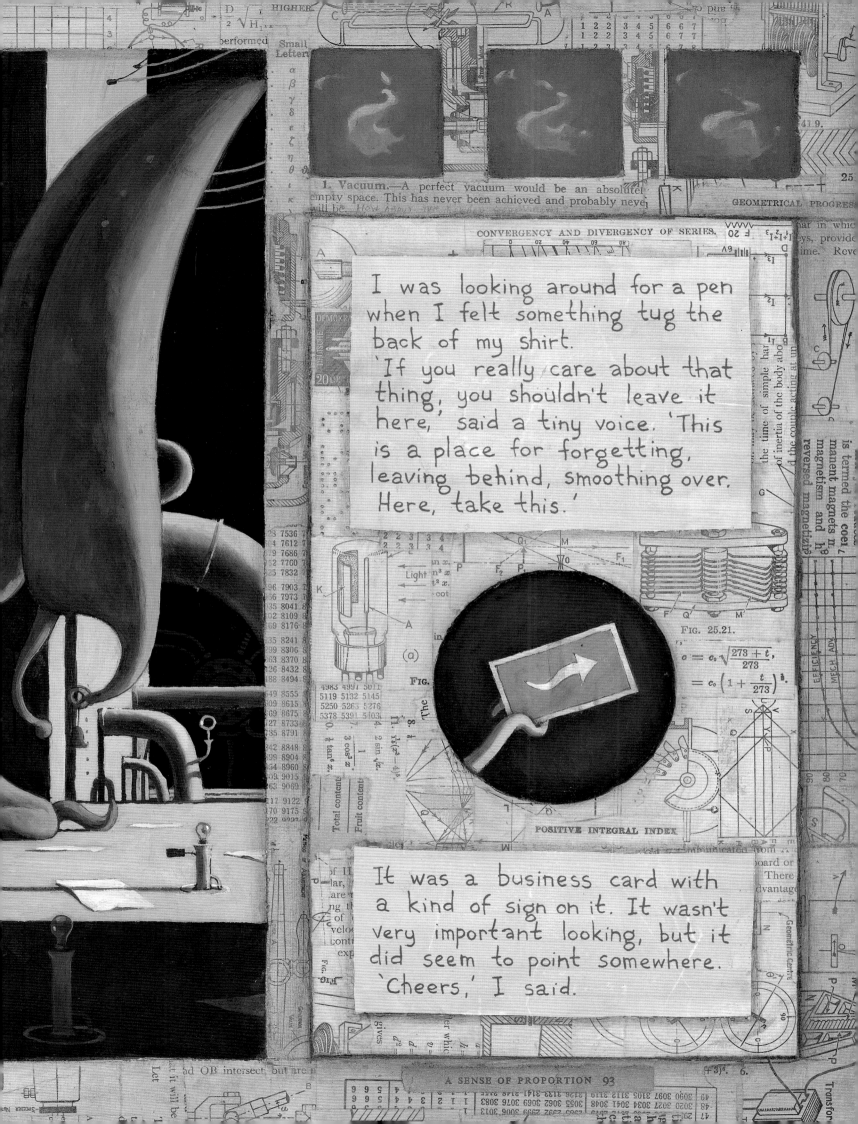

I was looking around for a pen when I felt something tug the back of my shirt.
'If you really care about that thing, you shouldn't leave it here,' said a tiny voice. 'This is a place for forgetting, leaving behind, smoothing over. Here, take this.'

It was a business card with a kind of sign on it. It wasn't very important looking, but it did seem to point somewhere.
'Cheers,' I said.

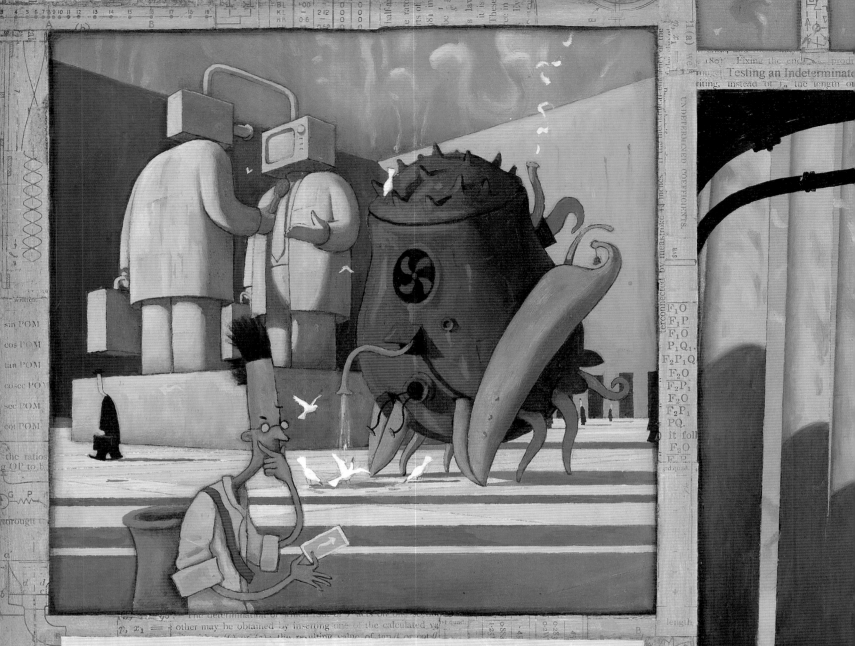

and hunted all over the place for this sign.

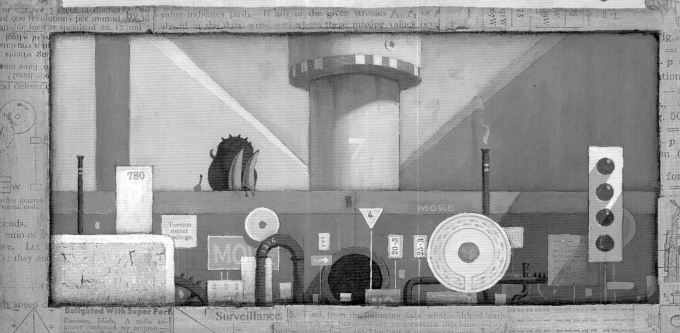

It wasn't an easy job,

and I can't say I knew what it all meant.

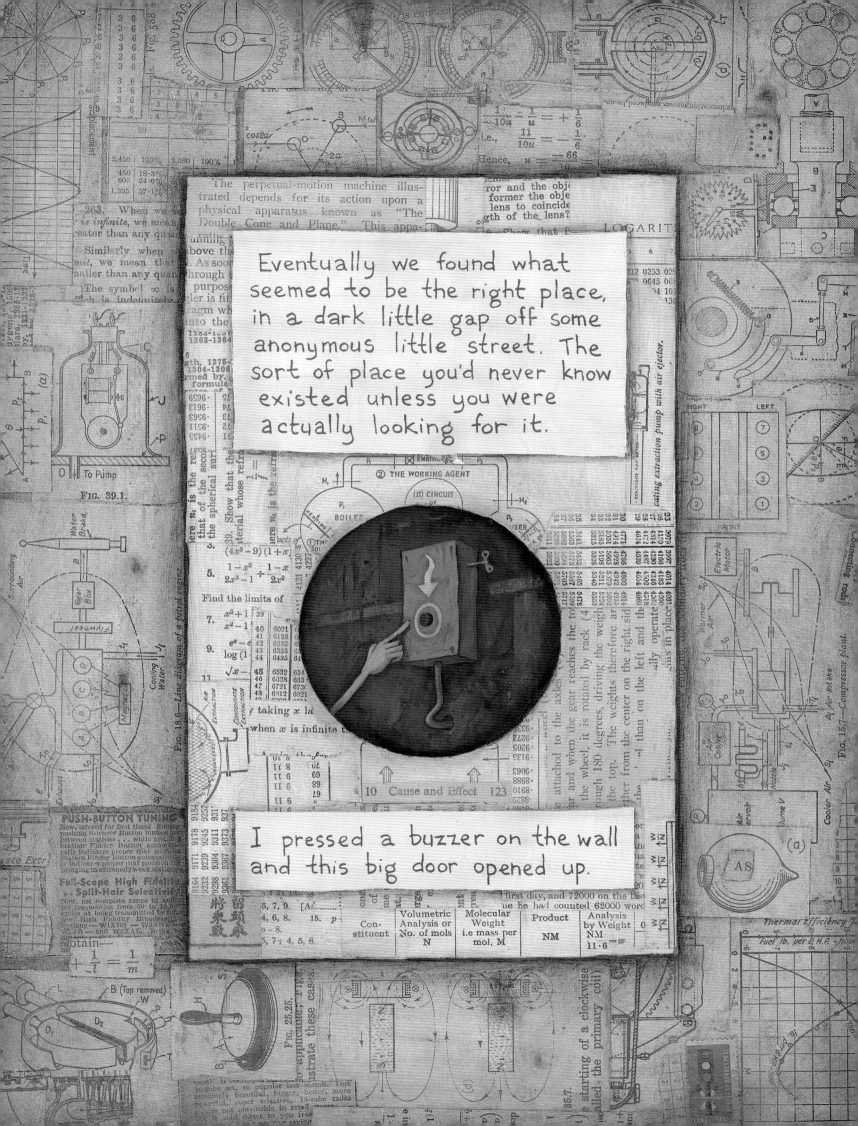

Eventually we found what seemed to be the right place, in a dark little gap off some anonymous little street. The sort of place you'd never know existed unless you were actually looking for it.

I pressed a buzzer on the wall and this big door opened up.

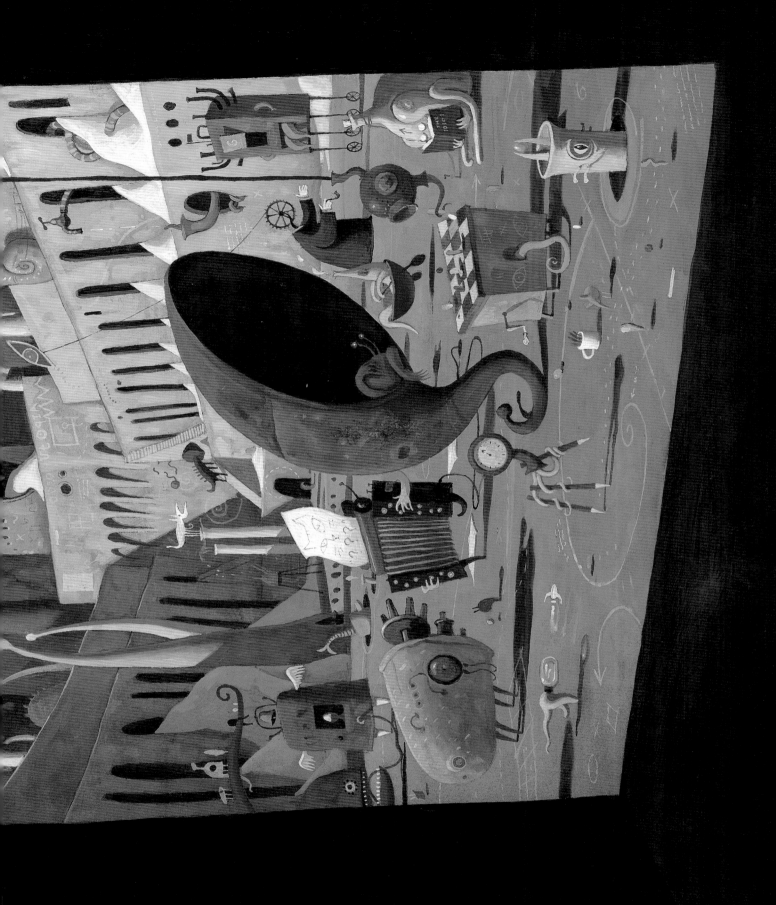

I didn't know what to think, but the lost thing made an approving sort of noise. It seemed as good a time as any to say goodbye to each other. So we did.

Then I went home to classify my bottle-top collection.

Well, that's it. That's the story.
Not especially profound, I know, but I
never said it was.
And don't ask me what the moral is.

I mean, I can't say that the thing
actually belonged in the place where it
ended up. In fact, none of the things
there really belonged. They all seemed
happy enough though, so maybe that
didn't matter. I don't know...

I still think about that lost thing from time to time. Especially when I see something out of the corner of my eye that doesn't quite fit.

You know, something with a weird, sad, lost sort of look.

I see that sort of thing less
and less these days though.

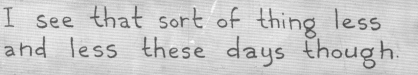

Maybe there aren't many lost
things around anymore.

Or maybe I've just stopped
noticing them.

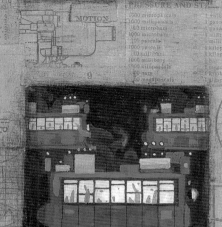

Too busy doing other stuff,
I guess.

Edward Hopper.

And APOLOGIES to Jeffrey Smart, & John Brack

Paul & The Twins.

The Funkmeister

Gary Crew,

BILL DAY,

centre folk,

the freo

and for valued interest and comments from Jonathan, Keira, Robin,

with THANKS to Helen Chamberlin

Chris D. a fellow connoisseur of heavy duty industrial plumbing

Editorial technician #264

the air in the clearance space should be made to expand reverse and adiabatically, but little can be done towards ensuring this